One minute, she had thought she was okay; and the next minute, her life just fell apart around her, fell *away* from her, like the sections of a tangerine when you put it down after removing the peel. . . .

. . .

"Brooks tells a very powerful story. Readers will feel to their very bones that it isn't Rex's dying that makes the difference to Alice but his living." (Starred review) —ALA *Booklist*

"A deeply felt, unusual, and absorbing story." —*School Library Journal*

"A trenchant and powerful fable." —*The Horn Book*

OTHER NOVELS BY BRUCE BROOKS

Asylum for Nightface

What Hearts

Everywhere

Midnight Hour Encores

The Moves Make the Man

VANISHING

BRUCE BROOKS

A Laura Geringer Book

Harper Tempest
An Imprint of HarperCollinsPublishers

Vanishing

Copyright © 1999 by Bruce Brooks

Library of Congress Cataloging-in-Publication Data
Brooks, Bruce.

Vanishing / Bruce Brooks.

p.   cm.

"A Laura Geringer book."

Summary: Eleven-year-old Alice is unwilling to return to live with her alcoholic mother
and her stern stepfather, so she refuses to eat to the point of slowly starving herself, in
order to remain in the hospital.

ISBN 0-06-028236-3. — ISBN 0-06-028237-1 (lib. bdg.) — ISBN 0-06-447234-5 (pbk.)
[1. Family problems—Fiction.   2. Emotional problems—Fiction.   3. Death—Fiction.
4. Hospitals—Fiction.]   I. Title.

PZ7.B7913Van   1999   99-11743
[Fic]—dc21   CIP

Typography by Hilary Zarycky

❖

First Harper Tempest edition, 2000

For Bill

VANISHING

She doesn't really remember the first time it happened. She knew only that she had left the surface of the bed beneath her and was slowly rising, until she reached a point where she stopped and simply hovered. She hung there, feeling surprised, but joyous, and lighter, definitely lighter. After a while she descended just as gently as she had risen, and she couldn't help feeling disappointed about going down. But the descent was not the quick flop gravity would have given her; no, she was still in the grip of something delicate and independent and strong.

The second time she found herself going a little higher, feeling a little lighter, a little more joyous. And this time she noticed the light above for the first time. It covered the ceiling, but seemed focused exactly above her, too pale to be bright, but intense and warm. It was a warmth she hadn't felt before—a welcoming warmth. But as she began her descent she knew she could only go as far up as she was taken, that she had to be lighter to rise higher, to reach that warmth.

Soon she found that she didn't need to wait for the rising experience to call her. This was quite startling at first—she wished for it, and it happened. Still she could only go as high as she was "allowed." She rose higher and higher. But the ceiling and the light were just out of reach. But she had learned to be patient; she knew she would get there.

She told the shrink and Rex about the rising and even about the lights. But she didn't tell them she could command the experience to start. This strange power of her will is her secret.

As the days passed, she noticed something new. Her skin was getting thinner. She was growing lighter and lighter—and transparent. She felt she could choose to pass through her skin from the inside, and then throw it away like a cellophane wrapper. But she could never quite bring herself to this, even though she felt "called" to do so. She was still too heavy, too heavy. On earth, she was so appallingly heavy. She was a burden to everyone.

Only Rex's voice could reach her when she was up.

Hearing it, she would always will herself down. Alice didn't know why Rex pulled her back, but one time he said, "They like you up there, don't they?" When Alice stammered some lame joke in reply, Rex shocked her by looking her earnestly in the eyes and saying, "Please, Al—I want you down here for a while. Promise me— don't fly away yet, okay?" Alice laughed, but when he insisted on the promise, she gave it. Now sometimes, up high, she almost regretted that promise.

ONE

WAITING ONLY A COUPLE of seconds for the air to settle a little after the doctor stormed from the room, Rex stretched in the institutional-green armchair like a waking cat and said, "Further evidence supporting my theory that *some*—not all, but *some*—people go to medical school because they get off on scaring other people, and see the unlimited possibilities that that M.D. and white coat give them."

"Don't I scare you, honey?" said the nurse with a mock pout. "I got a whole white *dress*." Rex gave a dismissive snort.

From the bed, where she was still going through something somewhere between an extended shudder and a bad case of the shivers, Alice managed to say, "Well, if he was out to scare *me*, he gets a 9.7, maybe a 9.8." For almost a week now she had been in the grips of a hallucination that let her *see* the words that came out of people's mouths—as something between pure light and brightly tinted plastic shapes. As her hallucinations went, it was one of the more amusing. She saw the fear in her voice now; she was talking in balloonlike, elongated, twisted ovals, silvery-gray and fading fast.

Rex looked at her keenly for a second. "You don't mean that coma stuff actually *got* to you?"

Alice tried to shrug, but it came off as an even bigger shudder. "It's possible my ability to scoff and blow off my doctor telling me I'm probably going to drop into a coma within twenty-four hours has been weakened a bit, by my having lost those famous thirty-two pounds he kept hammering on about."

"Don't need to hammer on—go look in a mirror, child," said the nurse. But Alice avoided mirrors.

Rex made another dismissive, mildly obscene mouth noise, which had a very brief but fascinating appearance to Alice—a series of bright-red bubbles that popped in descending order of size. "Comas are nothing special," he said. "As you know, I've—"

"—survived three of them in the past eighteen

months, yeah, yeah. You're the legendary Prince of Remission, well-known far and wide in the medical community for your miraculous hardiness in the face of a supposedly terminal disease and your fearless subjection to every experimental technique for a cure known to science. Whereas I am just a gal who won't eat, still subject to trifling fears at the idea of disappearing into a total lack of consciousness for an indefinite period, possibly forever." She tried a jaunty grin at Rex. "Remember, I didn't get into this thing to try to *die* or anything—"

"And all this time I thought your secret motivation was to keep me company as I wasted away," Rex sighed. "I had hoped this I-won't-go-home-and-be-unhappy business was just for show." He sighed again. "Another illusion about the brotherhood of man brutally shattered."

"It must be rough," said Alice. "If I were really your friend I would make sure I dropped dead at the exact moment you did."

"The exact moment I *do*," Rex corrected her grimly. He then said, "If you're afraid, try saying the word over and over again until it means nothing. That works for me sometimes. I just go *'Death Death Death Death . . .'* and pretty soon I might as well be saying *'Toast Toast Toast—'"* He clapped a hand over his mouth. "Oops. How tactless of me to mention food."

Alice tried it, repeating *Coma* eight times. Then she was silent.

"Well?" said Rex. "Are we better now?"

Alice shook her head. "Worse," she whispered.

"Okay, then try thinking of this: If you're in a coma, see, then that stepfather of yours can walk in here and, like, yell at you all he wants, and even threaten to swat you, and, like*, you won't even hear him! Because you'll be, like, in a coma, see!* Come on, man—it's *beautiful*, in its way." Rex gave a big fake smile that would have included highly raised eyebrows if he had possessed any, and nodded. "Now how's about *that* for some cheery thinkin'?"

"Gee, thanks," said Alice gravely.

Rex gave a disgusted wave. "Oh, then go ahead and *believe* your overdressed doctor-dude and be a fraidy-cat. 'Coma,'" he said in falsetto, rolling his eyes. "Oooooh, how vewy *fwightening*."

Alice looked out through her window, ignoring Rex. It was a winter morning. Lately she had been feeling as if she *were* a winter morning, all day, right there in her body: cold, dry, leafless, twiggy, but still very much alive, very much in motion. She *had* lost thirty-two pounds, and though she did not know it, she looked quite a bit like a dead tree with eyes.

In a few minutes, in a more sober voice, Rex said, "What part worries you, really? About the coma thing? Is it the idea of indefiniteness?"

It was a good question, one she had asked of herself many times. She believed she had never felt better. She also believed she spent most of her time hovering above the beds of the children's ward on a plateau of pure light.

"What scares me is the short-term memory loss he keeps mentioning as, like, a side effect."

"Oh, *that*." Rex waved a contemptuous hand. "It's probably a crock, and anyway who cares if you lose a little short-term memory?" He swept his arm around the empty ward. "You want to remember all *this*? Along with those fascinating visits from your mom, when she sits and reads a magazine article about putting the thrill back into her sex life while you think you're hovering up near the ceiling? Or the visits from *my* mom or dad, when they stand there for fifteen minutes with their hats in their hands like they were visiting a grave? These things you want to hang *on to*?" He suddenly laughed. "And most beautifully, when it comes to short-term memory, how are you even going to *know* what you lost? I mean, you won't *remember* what you—" He lost his sentence in laughter.

Alice nodded but didn't smile. After a moment she said, "Short-term memory is one of my best things. And it's also one of the more test-functional skills in intelligence measurement." She blinked to avoid entering a sheen of blue light that suddenly approached her through the window like weather, the distraction threatening to end this important conversation. She struggled to focus. "Because short-term memory is one of my strengths, I am loath to jeopardize—"

"Oh, come on. Listen to *you*—nobody is *ever* 'loath,' for one thing, so yank that one right out of the old vocabulary, Ms. Precious. And about these rumored tests—look, you're smart, or you're not, okay? Any test complex enough to claim to measure 'intelligence' is going to catch you *somewhere*. Of course," he added, with a melodramatic sniff, "there's a third option: You're smart, or you're not, or it could be that instead of these two you are dead, in which case the test form will sit blankly on the lonesome desk, all forlorn, a symbol of potential that will never be fulfilled, as is the case with poor old Rex." He sniffed a couple of times more, and sighed heavily. Alice knew it was not a sigh to be taken seriously.

"However," Rex continued, waving a hand, "*you*, with nothing *really* the matter with you—*you* have a future to worry about, looking ahead to which law schools might look askance at those short-term memory scores a few years back—"

"I'm not going to be a lawyer and you know it," said Alice, "and anyway you've lasted here almost eighteen months. Why should we suppose you're going to succumb to your cruel illness anytime soon, leaving that desk unoccupied and that form blank and that potential unfulfilled? How do we know anything's really wrong with you, except that you're going bald? Yeah—you could be faking this whole thing just to get a little special attention." Alice laughed and, as she did so, she looked again out the window and wondered where the curtain of blue light had gone.

"Jeez, I think I *am* getting bored," Rex announced. He hauled himself out of his chair.

"So learn Japanese. I hear it's challenging," said Alice. "Build small ships in bottles using only period wood and cloth. Write some sonnets. Write some sonnets in *Japanese*. Recover intact from another couple of comas, then recover from your secret fatal disease. You have lots of options."

"There was a nurse from Japan on the ward

once," Rex said, sitting back into the chair again, sideways, and putting his hands behind his head. "Some stupid exchange program, a sister hospital in Osaka or somewhere. But we had one slight problem with this particular student: She spoke absolutely no English. Not one word—not 'yes' or 'no' or 'spinal meningitis' or anything. So naturally they assigned her to the *children's* ward, because you don't need to *talk* to kids, right? Well, one of the guys in here, I swear I'm telling the truth, he was this brand-new amputee who'd got his foot caught in a combine or something, working his daddy's tobacco farm, and it was all he thought about, the farm I mean, not the injury, he just completely blew off the amputation of one of his two feet as if a prosthesis were an expected fringe benefit from the work. This kid had this tobacco-toolbook. Ah, what a book it was. A master-piece, Alice. With good-quality photographs, printed perfectly on excellent paper. It was this mouthwater-ing catalogue of tobacco-harvesting equipment, if you can imagine such a thing. It had *scads* of, like, really obscure stuff, very peculiar-looking machinery, many pieces of which you could easily imagine chew-ing this kid's foot up, snicker-snack." Rex smiled. "So in six weeks we taught this Japanese nurse every-thing in this book—every word to go with every picture of every obscure tobacco tool. Functions, too! She was a one-woman smoke-farm staff. Then she left, and we never heard from her again. But I bet she's a real hit at parties in Osaka."

"She probably is," said Alice, trying to maintain her concentration through Rex's long story. Sometimes, during hallucinations, she found it troublesome to bring her attention back to Rex. "The Japanese smoke almost as much as the Americans do."

"There you are, then. With their talent-spotting system, they've probably nailed her by now and made her Minister of Amputation and Carcinoma."

"But let's get back to my coma."

Rex was impatient. "Look, *what* coma? Doctors just fling these words around." Acting disgusted, he nevertheless rattled off a series of quick questions. "Do you feel suddenly and unusually faint?"

"No. Just kind of lightheaded, as usual. Pleasant, actually. Very *clear*."

"Clear, shmeer. You're probably about two missed glucose drops from acute induced psychosis, you know. But coma? Do you fall asleep at odd times— drifting off into sudden deep naps, waking up not knowing where you are, that kind of thing?"

"No," said Alice. "I hardly sleep at all. I—I just kind of shimmer beneath the sheets, see, and sort of glow through the night." She blushed.

Rex rolled his eyes. "You're entirely too poetic—and too *bad* at it—to be *really* sick, which is why you've had to go and invent an illness just for yourself. 'I just kind of shimmer!'" Then Rex laughed and shook his head. "But see, that's what's got these docs so mad! You 'just kind of shimmer'—what are they supposed to do with *that*? You are in complete control! They're flat out of their league when it comes to you, no predictions leading to exact results, no surgical removals, no treatment schedules. You—only you—are the boss, the inventor. It all waits on you—the Honcho. The Hog. You, Alice, are the *man*."

"Yeah," said Alice, and for the first time, still looking out the window, at a landscape wrapped again in blue like a present, she smiled. "I am. I am the *man*."

TWO

$\int$IX WEEKS INTO HER hunger strike, Alice was in the state she supposed could be called "dozing," though to her that word seemed all too unconscious, too dull. To be accurate: She felt as if she were hovering a few inches up, with a bright light beneath her body holding her aloft, and a brighter one beckoning from the ceiling. Even when her mother entered the room, the state was not dispelled.

Alice turned her face toward her mother, gave her a polite smile. Her mother always looked at Alice now as if the girl were someone else, a stranger she was assigned to spend half an hour with despite the lack of anything between them. She never spoke to Alice at all anymore. She had been this way since about the third week of Alice's strike, when her pleas—"a mother's pleas," as she never ceased to remind the girl and anyone else within hearing—had failed. Now she sank with a show of wounded silence into the green chair, opened her purse, and took out a magazine already rolled open to a story. Glancing again at Alice, her mother crossed her legs and read. This is the way her visits went, now; after half an hour of silent reading, she would put the magazine back in her purse, stand up, walk over to plant a dry, alcohol-stinky kiss somewhere on Alice's forehead, then leave without a word.

Alice supposed her mom had reason to be angry. As she had put it shortly after the girl announced her hunger strike and proved she was serious about it, "You mean you'd rather starve yourself to death than come home with me."

Alice had tried to correct the melodramatic "to death" but had been drowned out in a flood of self-pitying grief.

And now, here her mother was, dutifully visiting Alice as she wasted away, letting her anger show in silence. Yet she showed Alice respect by choosing not to drink from her nickel-plated hip flask in the starving girl's presence. Alice appreciated the gesture too much to tell her mother that she stank anyway. The skinnier Alice got, the better she could see, hear, taste, feel the touch of things, and smell.

Though she had not needed that sharpness to detect the metabolized-liquor smell of her mother when she woke up during her ambulance ride from the airport seven weeks before. It was strong, and it was very close to Alice's face. "My baby! My baby-doll!" her mother kept repeating.

Alice had opened her eyes to find that she was lying on her back, strapped to a small bed, in a truck full of medical gear. An attendant dressed in white was standing near the rear doors, pointedly looking away. Yes. Alice was back. Back with mom.

Alice had closed her eyes again, and once more passed out.

It must have been quite a while before she regained consciousness. When she next opened her eyes she was in a bed once more, but a normal one, in a very large room full of beds, all unoccupied. And she was staring into the face of a boy without a hair on his head, not even eyebrows. His face was not a foot from Alice's, and it bore a studious, appraising expression. Almost as soon as Alice opened her eyes and wrinkled her forehead at the rudeness, the face pulled back and the studious expression turned into a grin.

"I'm Rex," said the boy. "I'm supposed to be dead, but I'm not. And it's a good thing you're as young as me—if we were older they wouldn't let us sleep in the same ward on account of, you know. . . ."

The boy's breath fluttered over Alice's face like wind waving through oats. He went on.

"I'm kind of the unofficial union representative for the kids' side of things in this place," he said. "Unofficial because of course the kids, in fact no one group of patients, has, like, a *union* or anything. But unless somebody keeps all these brilliant docs and Ph.D. administrators aware that they *have* kids in here, they'd treat us the way everybody outside treats us—like 'lesser people,' you know? Not just like 'younger people.'"

"Wow," said Alice. All she could think to say, besides that, was, "Thanks. For the representation." She cleared her throat. It hurt. But she noticed the impulse to cough receded. "Have you gotten anything, like, passed into law so far?"

"Indeed we have," said Rex. "Thanks to our— that is to say, *my*—untiring efforts, the dietitian is no longer allowed to serve us any combination of tapioca and Jell-O as our dessert more than twice a week." He winced a little. "I hate tapioca—it's like eating the eyeballs of a small animal. And the Jell-O is always yellow with brown banana slices suspended in it."

"Yuck."

"And now we have a lot more layer cake and pie," said Rex proudly.

"Much better," said Alice. She looked around the huge ward but saw only two other beds showing signs of occupation. One stood directly beneath the high windows that made up a kind of gallery in the old building's wards; it looked well lived-in, an easy chair angled away from it with a floor lamp beside the chair, and two wooden bookcases holding mostly books interspersed with snack packages running along the other side of the bed. This, Alice decided, had to be Rex's bailiwick.

The other occupied bed was way off in a much darker corner of the room. It seemed to hold someone's bad-joke idea of The Mummy.

"That's Robert Pendergrass, who likes to be called Robert but whom I have nicknamed Bobby Q. in light of his situation, which is that he is badly burned over eighty per cent of his body. His clothes caught fire from the candles on his birthday cake. All he says, if he hears you approach, is, 'I got me an

Erector set. With a *motor*.'" Rex shook his head sadly.

"Are you acting all tender-hearted because he's likely to die or because his conversation is so dull?" asked Alice, who thought the nickname cruel, but clever.

"Both," said Rex. Then he looked Alice dead in the eye and frowned. "And don't think the two things are not related. I have found a much higher survival rate among those who keep their wits sharp—and, of course, who have wits in the first place. The dulling drugs they give you are a greater challenge than any illness—"

"Look out," said the nurse. "Here comes Mr. Wonderful."

"Nattering on about the nasty meds again, Rex?" said a young doctor who seemed to blow in from nowhere, borne on a brisk wind of professional good health. He was wearing a white coat, a pale-blue shirt that reminded Alice of deep bathwater, and a paisley tie that looked to her like what one might see if one looked at some nasty culture of viruses beneath a microscope.

"Bad bronchitis, *bad*," said the man, perching a hip on Alice's bed as Rex retired to his own nook quickly, muttering to himself. The doctor spoke fiercely with the cutting quality of sleet. "A touch of pneumonia too. Starting to spike a *very* nasty fever. The bronch was quite far along. Were you even seen by a physish wherever you were?"

Alice, who despised people who spoke in abbreviations, said, "Yes, but I think he was used to a simpler pediatric practice."

"Well, he sure as the dickens missed this bronchitis, and it was obvious enough that a first-year med student could have diagnosed it," said the jaunty doctor coolly. He jacked himself off Alice's bed. "Gotcha now, though, and got that bad stuff in there too. You're weak as an earthworm in a parking lot, so we're keeping you until we can fatten you up, get that pulmonary circulation back to where it should be for an active eleven-year-old, then we'll bid you adieu. But you'll be around for a while yet, long enough for Rex over there to talk you into picketing for more kids' magazines in the waiting room." He smacked Alice on the side hard enough for the blow to sting slightly, as if to show *he* was no sexist, then winked as if he *were*, after all. Alice also despised people who presumed to wink at her.

"See you soon. Eat your nice meals," said the doctor, and blew out of the room, taking the cold blast with him.

"Be still, my heart," said the nurse.

Alice called across to Rex, who was sitting in his armchair with the floor lamp casting a yellow glow on the thick book he was reading.

"How come *you* weren't honored with a visit from the good doctor?"

Without looking up from his book, Rex said, "They don't bother with me anymore. Just waiting for my unexpected remission to stutter and stop so I'll die like I'm supposed to. Besides, that guy's a pulmonary specialist, and my problem isn't in my lungs."

"Where *is* your problem?" asked Alice. "What do you have, anyway?"

Rex closed his book with a loud slap. "That," he said, "is my little secret. Suffice to say it's in a place the doctors consider buried beyond hope, buried so deep they won't go after it with their knives."

"So it's fatal? You're, like, a terminal case?"

"So I am told," said Rex. But he put both hands outward to display his relaxed, cross-legged posture. "But as you see, medical guesswork *could* be wrong."

"Do your parents believe the doctors?"

Rex sighed heavily, got up from his chair, and carefully replaced the book on the shelves. 'Believe' is hardly the word," he said as he moved. "Something more like 'embrace' covers it better."

"Come on! No parents want to hear their son is dying! You can't say that."

"No, maybe not," said Rex, turning, sticking his hands in the pockets of his robe, and strolling back toward Alice. "But some people are so eager to believe the worst—about anything—and when you take those people and put the 'worst' in the mouth of a physician—then you get the kind of fatalism that afflicts my mom and dad."

"But they visit you," said Alice.

"As little as possible, and when they're here they're not *really* here, if you know what I mean," said Rex, hiking himself up to sit on the foot of Alice's bed. "It's all right, though. See, when the doctor told us I had this fatal thing, I happened to be watching their faces, and I *saw*, I *saw* that for them I really died right then. I was gone from that point on, a dead man. And I understood! Then this huge remission hit."

Rex nodded toward the bandaged form in the other bed. "Bobby Q will be gone soon, and it's terrible to see how torn up his mom and dad are when they come. I'd much rather have my mom."

"Do you have to call him that?"

"Yes, I do, and you have to call me Rex, which isn't my real name either but which I figured I'd adopt, because I always wanted to be called Rex." He put a hand to his chin and considered Alice. "Now the question is, what do we call you?"

"Alice is bad enough."

"Ah. Because of the white rabbit and the hole and the Queen of Hearts and all that?"

"Say 'Off with her head!' once and I'll punch you right in your secret spot."

Rex rubbed his chin, closed one eye, and thought. "Wait—wasn't there another Alice, in the Pooh stories?"

"There was not, so don't even try," Alice said. "The whole lot was a shocking mess of homily, except for Eeyore. Say a word against Eeyore and you get punched again, twice as hard."

Rex's face lit up like a hundred-watt bulb, which, in fact, his head resembled. "Ah, the consistent crankiness of Eeyore, who serves as the only relief to the sappiness of the Hundred Acre Wood, where you'll notice, no predators ever prey—I mean, Owl never rips Rabbit's leg off for dinner or anything. Still, I can't see calling you Eeyore."

"Don't you dare. I don't deserve the honor. And the word is funny to say, makes you sound like you're braying, though I can't see Eeyore actually braying."

"Maybe we'll leave it at Alice for now—but you

can't escape the Looking-Glass reference, you know."

"*Must* a nickname be cruel?" Alice said.

"Absolutely," said Rex, "unless it's mine, because I am a poor dying boy."

"You look pretty healthy to me," said Alice skeptically. "You could shave all that hair off pretty easily and fake it."

Rex scoffed. "A thinly disguised ploy to learn my secret illness. No, I have X rays to prove my malady, as much as an X ray can 'prove' anything, and I'll be happy to wave them at you from across the room, pointing out the offending tissue, which is quite easy to see."

"How would I know they're not some poor dead golden retriever's X rays or something?"

Rex sighed. "Maybe you'll get lucky and I'll drop dead before you leave, obliterating all doubts."

"Actually, I believe you," Alice said more soberly.

"That's fine," said Rex, "but let's not get morose about it. In the meantime, it's not a bad life—no school, all the books I want, an occasional painkiller if I feel like getting a buzz on."

"And you're famous. First thing, a nurse showed me this article in a bigtime medical journal—"

Rex winced. "Oh, yes—the 'Prince of Remission' and all that crap."

Alice half smirked. "You don't like being famous?"

Rex looked a little sheepish. "Well, if there weren't any ballyhoo, maybe God would kind of forget about me and I'd just keep going on and on and on. . . ."

"So you believe in God?"

"I do not."

"But you just said—"

"If someone told you you had a fatal disease at age eleven, something you had done *nothing* to catch, would *you* believe in this benevolent God everybody talks about? Because that's the only flavor he comes in—kind, good. You don't hear anybody talking about a God who toys cruelly with people and takes children's lives at a whim, do you?"

Alice, seeing it was a complicated matter, merely shrugged.

"But I have a good fighting *spirit*, my lass," Rex said, tapping Alice on the leg. "I learned it from all of the World War Two movies. You know—'They'll never take me alive!' My plane is flying until the instant it hits the sea in a burst of flame. I hear trumpets and violins in major chords. And I say, 'What the heck do they really know, anyway?'"

THREE

THE NEXT EVENING, Alice's mother paid a visit to the ward. She was drunk. "And how's my darling today?" she asked Rex, who was perched at the foot of Alice's bed.

"I'm going to die," Rex said, and Alice's mother's face fell.

"But they said—"

"I'm up here, Mom," said Alice, and her mother swung her head as if it were a ball on the end of a tether. "That's my friend Rex."

"Alice!" her mother said, looking at her, then back at Rex. "You're not Alice! You're bald!"

"And you're not Minnie Mouse," said Rex with a nice smile.

"Course not." She swung her head back so she was looking at Alice. "How's my little—"

"Is Nat in the car downstairs? Did Nat drive?" Alice asked.

"Nat," said her mother. "Downstairs. Love to visit, no parking—"

"I just wanted to make sure someone was driving you," said Alice. "It's quite all right that he doesn't come himself."

"Bronchitis, easy, no problem," said her mother as a nurse appeared in the doorway and looked at Alice. Alice nodded. The nurse put a steadying hand on her mother's forearm.

"Let's go see Nat," the nurse said.

"Love to visit," Alice's mother said.

"I'm sure," said Alice. "Mother, it was nice of you to come, but really it would be best if you came, say, during your lunch break from work or—"

The nurse was leading her toward the hallway and, one assumed, the elevators.

"Darling Alice, my baby, bronchitis, easy."

"Yes, Mom," said Alice. "It will all be easy."

With that, her mother and the nurse disappeared through the swinging doors.

"It will all most certainly *not* be easy," said Rex. "I'm sorry."

Alice said nothing for a few moments, then she shrugged. "I don't see any reason I can't get around it pretty easy—me, I mean. I mean, it's not *me* who drinks."

"It's not I," Rex corrected involuntarily. "But don't shrug it off, buddy. The alcohol doesn't have to be in your veins to be in your life."

"You sound like an Al-Anon poster," said Alice.

"Ouch," said Rex, springing off the bed and heading back to his chair. "You know how to hurt a guy. A poster!"

"Not just any poster—an *Al-Anon* poster, and they don't *get* any more goody-goody than that."

"Go ahead—wound me. Take out all of that repressed anger on poor old—"

"I am not angry," said Alice through clenched teeth.

"No?" said Rex, dropping into his chair with his book again. "Then we'll just say you're 'compassionate.' How's that?"

Alice didn't reply. After a moment, Rex looked down at his book and resumed his reading.

But Alice had a last thing to say, and it took her several minutes. "And Rex?" she said in a quiet voice.

Rex looked up. "Yes, Alice?"

"The Minnie Mouse thing? Just . . . just don't

ever play with her when she's drunk. Don't *toy* with her when she's that bad."

Rex seemed to consider, then he nodded. "Fair enough," he said. "But I'm curious—what would you do if I did?"

"I'd make you look like Bobby Q over th—where is he?"

Rex gazed at the ceiling. In a much softer voice, he said, "Bobby Q checked out last night." He started swinging his foot, letting the leather heel of his slipper slap his skin. "Cleared him out by two a.m. Here less than two weeks, first sign of a crisis, *poof!* Gone! I tell you, Alice, they don't make them with grit anymore, no staying power, no fire in the belly. The way they make them now, they keel over and die first chance they get."

Alice said, "Robert was in a lot of pain, Rex. Cut him some slack for checking out on you."

"It so happens Bobby Q was enjoying the very finest selection of painkilling medication this hospital has to offer," said Rex, who made a habit of reading the charts of other patients, "so don't waste your sympathy. He was stoned to the ears, *all* the time. That may have been the problem—the boy just felt too good. In any case, the trouble, as it so often is, was that he simply did not know how *not* to give up.

He did not know you must resist, you must not let the suckers, either inside or outside, kill your ass just because they *say* your ass is supposed to get killed."

"*Nobody's* supposed to get *killed*," said Alice.

FOUR

IT REALLY HAD BEEN just a matter of minutes. One minute, she had thought she was okay; and the next minute, her life just fell apart around her, fell *away* from her, like the sections of a tangerine when you put it down after removing the peel. One minute she was living with her father, admittedly with her grandmother too, and Alice knew her coughing at night got on Nana's nerves, but still . . . then the next minute her grandmother was running down the stairs out into the rain screaming "I can't stand it!" and the back door slammed, and Alice heard her dad chasing after her grandmother, right up to the second slamming of the door. The next thing she knew, the door opened, only once and quietly.

She heard her grandmother's voice, indistinct, but sounding snappish and firm. Then her father's voice came in, speaking longer, sounding kind of pleading, but her grandmother cut him off with another snap. That was all Alice heard. Then she watched as her dad, with his hair all wet and droplets running down one side of his nose, came into her room and sat heavily on the end of her bed—without regard for getting the bedclothes wet.

His carelessness set off an alarm in Alice a second before it was answered. Alice would no longer be living there, he said. That was it. That fast. No questions, no tests, no arguments. Then he started to babble a little—about how it had been an "experiment" and it "just wasn't working out" with Nana, she was a little touchy maybe, Pops had been dead only six months, she had trouble sleeping as it was and it wasn't like they could find any legitimate reason Alice kept up with that coughing business. . . .

Her father apparently thought that was all he had to do, deliver the news, because he rose like some sopping retriever and made as if to move off. But Alice had a few things to say, and she froze her father standing at the foot of her bed, with the first.

"If you send me back I'll die, Dad."

His brow wrinkled, and Alice realized that what he saw as melodrama had angered him, given him an out, so she hastened to clarify.

"Mom is drinking. She drinks every day, and she still drives everywhere. But most of all"—and she knew this was the hardest point to make in terms of *danger*, this was the hardest to get across as being perilous to the point of some possible, unforeseen fatality—"this guy she married, Dad, he's, he's, he *hates* me, sets tests I can only flunk, and he makes me *pay*, Dad, he makes me pay in ways that will add up, they *will*, they will add up and someday they will kill me, I swear."

Her father had stood, dripping and frowning, listening to this. He thought for a long moment, then spoke to Alice in a false voice, an Adult Addressing His Child voice, which was never how he talked.

"I am sorry, Alice. But I cannot exactly say I am surprised, you know? I mean, your mother *would* pick someone completely unlike me. She, frankly, found me weak. Wimpy, she used to say. So I am not shocked to hear she has chosen—well, a man so 'strong' that he might at times seem threatening to you. A bully. But—"

"He *has* threatened me, though. It's not my imagination. See, he—" Alice tried to break in, but her father overrode her.

"—but I have every faith, if not in your mom or her mate, at least in *you*, Alice. And I know *you* can work out some sort of . . . truce. You can deal with challenges. You've dealt with your share already."

"Well, if I've dealt with my share already, why do I have to deal with this one too?"

"Don't get sassy," said her father, dripping, and looking down for the first time at the rug as it turned wet. "Look, I've got to change." And he left.

"I'll die," Alice called after him. "You're killing me."

"Nonsense," came her father's voice from the hallway, receding. "You're too smart—sorry, but you've already proved it."

"And you—you've just proved you're *dense*, Dad. And wimpy, just like Mom said." Almost before she knew it, she hopped out of bed and ran to the dormer window in her room and opened it. She vaulted onto the windowsill; it was still raining hard outside. The slates that made up the roof looked slick and shiny, and she had the urge to touch them with her bare feet. She climbed out. The slates were wet and cold. She took a couple of steps, keeping her left hand behind her on the outside corner of the windowsill. She just managed to peek forward over the edge of the gutter to see the iron railing of the front porch below, when all at once her arm was caught from behind, and with more roughness than she had ever felt, she was yanked, in almost one motion, off the roof and back over the sill, then dumped onto the floor.

Her father was standing over her, shaking with some emotion she had never seen before. He was panting, which made his words difficult to understand. He pointed one finger in her face, and said, between pants, ". . . Scare . . . take you seriously . . . stunt like that . . ." Finally he dropped his finger, stopped trying to pant his way through his message, and, still panting, barked out one commanding word: "Pack."

She packed, quickly.

Her father hustled her out of the house so fast Alice never even got to say good-bye to her grandmother. Whizzing by the kitchen door Alice looked in and saw Nana with her forehead in her hands and a strand of wet gray hair hanging down to within a half-inch of the surface of her steaming cup. Alice supposed her grandmother had no special interest in saying good-bye—she wasn't eager to have the guilt spelled out, though Alice could see she already felt it. Good.

On the drive through the rain to the airport, Alice tried to talk normally, but her father said nothing. Alice noticed that her dad had put on a shirt and tie and blazer and slacks, though. He looked businesslike, as though nothing about this speeding trip in the darkness to the airport was abnormal at all. Somewhere in the rush through the terminal, Alice's legs just gave out, stopped following her orders. It was the oddest thing. She suddenly realized how terribly bad she felt physically—her head kept spinning. It wouldn't stop, the spinning, and it threw all her other senses into disarray, so that she hardly knew she had been dragged and bundled onto the plane and explained to the flight crew and placed carefully into a seat and belted in. Her father's face, strangely smiling, bobbed in front of her, then was gone. There was speed then, and force pressing her backwards as always, and then everything felt startlingly free and soft and high, and Alice closed her eyes.

She woke to find three people, two women in blue uniforms and a man in a white shirt with military epaulets, feeling her head and peering at her. Alice noticed she was wet with perspiration beneath her clothes, but she was cold too.

She tried to speak, to say the words, "I will never

cough again, I promise," but just opening her mouth made her start hacking, and she could not seem to stop. She heard the man say, "I'd guess at least 104, and just listen to *that*. I'll radio ahead to have an ambulance meet us." The women nodded, and looked at Alice as if from afar.

Alice kept trying to promise, but all she could do was cough, and cough, and cough. What was happening to her will, anyway? To her anger, her sense of doom? Eventually, without meaning to, she passed out.

Now, from the foot of her hospital bed, her mother turned suddenly and looked at her hard, eyes flashing like bright copper.

"One thing," she said, smiling tightly at Alice. "Your father had *his* chance."

"What do you mean?"

"He'll never get you again," her mother nearly crowed. "Oh, yes, he was wonderful at playing with blocks and walking in the woods and reading the storybooks with you on his knee—all the *easy* things when you were little. But when the going gets rough, when my darling is almost dying, all he can think of is pleasing his momma and sticking his own sick girl on a *plane*."

Alice tried to glower back, but fell short and

instead gave off only a kind of defensive glimmer. Who knew better than she that her father had managed to grasp her only weakly this time—that he had dropped her like a poorly thrown pass? She felt her throat nearly close—not with the bronchitis—and her eyes filled. But without crying, she told her mother, "You don't understand. You weren't there."

"Lucky for him!"

"But he *did* try to help me," said Alice. "He—he got me a doctor. It was just—the doctor didn't see what was wrong with me. That's not Daddy's fault. And—well, when I sort of collapsed in the airport—well, you see, I had done something kind of stupid back at the house, and Daddy probably thought, I don't know, that I was faking or hysterical or something, and he should force me to just, you know, 'soldier on.'" She looked at her mother, whose stare had not softened. "Well, *I* don't blame him," she said defiantly.

"Maybe not, but I can promise you he won't be getting anywhere near you now," her mother said.

"But—"

"He won't even try to come," said her mother. "I've let him know there's no point in trying. If he does, he'll get no further than the main desk. So don't you worry about it."

Alice closed her eyes. She could think of nothing to say. What was the point? Maybe her mother was right. She had to face it. Maybe for her father, she *was* history.

FIVE

She wakes and finds she is a simple, egg-shaped bubble. Her size hasn't changed, but as soon as she notices this, the bubble begins to shrink. Smaller she gets, and smaller still, and she notices, as the speed picks up, that with the loss of size comes a terrible increase in pressure, pressure she cannot escape. Faster. She is the size of a beach ball, an orange, a marble. The pressure—surely she will explode. A match head, a speck of dust, and smaller though a bubble still, a point. Then suddenly the bubble collapses on itself and she is released into a smallness that is nothing at all.

SIX

HALF A YEAR BEFORE, Alice's mother had married a man named Nat, marking a definite finish to her previous marriage to Alice's dad and their life in Washington, as well as establishing a new shape for the family. The new guy was someone Alice's mom had known long before, when they went to high school together in this, her hometown. He now worked as an automobile mechanic. He smoked Pall Malls. He went to visit his mother every day across town. He attended church five times a week, along with the new members of his family. He insisted on what Alice could only suppose was an old-style Southern code of manners, giving her a quick swat across the cheeks if she failed to end any sentence addressed to an elder with either the word 'Sir' or 'Ma'am'.

Otherwise Alice didn't know a whole lot about her new stepfather. The one time she had tried to engage him in conversation by asking some fairly intelligent questions about a clutch plate or something, he had removed his cigarette from his mouth for just long enough to give her a sideways look and say, "I mind my work, you mind yours." And that was that.

Her stepfather, though, was beside the point. What had really been important during those months, and the months of separation from her real father preceding them, had been Alice's sudden susceptibility to seizures of spontaneous weeping—deep, sucking sobs that doubled her over, and had teachers rushing her from class, her mother rushing her from church, and her new cousins staring mutely at her in the middle of the pickup softball games they were nice enough to let her join. Also, Alice would find herself literally prone to what she called "fallings" into the gloomiest of lethargies (fits was too nutty a word), sometimes lasting four or five days, during which she curled up in her bed and could not bring herself to move—not to eat, not to watch

The Simpsons, not to go to school or church or soft-ball. She was too heavy to move, as if her body were made of stone. When her mother would ask what was wrong, Alice would always say, "I miss him." She meant her father, of course, whom she'd seen for only two weeks in the summer, back in Washington.

Her stepfather let it be known that he wasn't pay-ing good money for any "nuts" in his house to go con-sult "nut doctors," no matter how bad their behavior was. Alice was left to wend her own way back to nor-mal, which she always did. But several months of this stuff annoyed Alice herself every bit as much as it annoyed Nat. The crying and the bedridden times—and the stated reason for them—got to Alice's mom, too, pinning her between her daughter and the man she had married. Drinking more and more, handling Alice less and less well, unable to figure out a way to fit the girl comfortably into her new life, pressed by the man Alice called "Sergeant Husband" to by God *be* his wife and not just a nurse to her snively weirdo of a kid, finally, one day, she offered to let Alice leave Nat's house and go live with her father.

The truth was, Alice's mother, through her boozy haze, understood her daughter's grieving. She knew these periods of morbid distemper had their roots in the special affinity she had witnessed, unfortunately from the outside, as it sprang up between daughter and father before they were ripped apart.

Alice's memories of being a small girl almost all contained her father as the parent who understood her. The fact is, Alice had sensed very early that in some strange way she simply frightened her mother; not as a threat, because from the beginning she had been the most peacefully investigative of girls, but rather, as an alien.

Alice recalled that when she talked with her father, they simply talked—no big deal. Alice asked what she wanted to know, or offered an observation she wanted to share, and her dad replied. Or, sometimes, her father was the one who initiated the question or observation. In any case, it was always felt like equal-to-equal. Whereas Alice was always aware of *addressing* her mother. Often, a flash of alarm would pass through her mom's eyes that Alice interpreted as meaning "What is she going to ask of me? Can I handle it?" And her talks with her mom rarely did more than hang in the air. She felt it, and she knew her mother did, too.

It wasn't until Alice learned—abruptly, from her mother—that her dad had already gone to some nameless netherland where fathers awaiting divorce were apparently banished, that she could ever have imagined such a perverse arrangement. Whose idea had *this* been? She could not picture either of her parents coming up with it, and secretly remained convinced it had been the idea of some stupid judge.

During her year of waiting for the divorce, Alice's mother had made an honest and hardy effort to "get" her. But she had been hindered by the almost constant presence of Nat, who ate dinner with them every night and sat watching television while Alice's mom tried to keep up with her daughter's schoolwork. Nat plainly considered Alice practically a Martian, and he made no effort whatsoever to win the girl over as he courted her mother.

Meanwhile, for two weeks that summer she was allowed to visit her father, who had set up a rather pitiful lone life in a little apartment. But there were signs the pitiful nature of the life—the loneliness, perhaps—would be changing. Her dad had bought, for example, a small but potent stereo and a bunch of CDs, several of which Alice identified as either schmaltzy-romantic in nature, or "swinging bachelor-pad" jazz.

During the mornings, afternoons, and evenings, his attention belonged to Alice. Once in a while during the day they would need to run an errand, mostly having to do with his place (buying curtain rods and curtains, or a new toaster, or music). Before setting out on such forays, her dad always asked in a rather courtly manner if Alice minded spending a little of their time on such mundane chores. Of course she never minded—she was with her dad, that was all that mattered.

When the two weeks were up, Alice and her dad parted with a see-you-soon casualness that seemed to assume the easiness of future contact. It was shortly after she had returned to her mother and Nat that her weird spells began.

Then her mother's offer of salvation had come. Go live with Dad? Alice accepted it immediately, of course; within an hour she was packed and ready for the trip to the airport, while her mother made all of the arrangements with her father over the telephone. There was a moment when Alice found herself alone with Nat, and, in her bliss, she got up the gumption to say, "You couldn't possibly think I've been acting this way on *purpose*, as if I find it somehow *fun* or something? I—I don't even *understand* it!"

Nat took a drag of his Pall Mall and expelled the smoke hard through his nostrils. "Then why in heck did you *do* it?" he said.

Alice had just shaken her head, insolence which would have previously earned her a smack across the cheek according to her stepfather's moral code, but which went unpunished now. What was the point? She knew perfectly well Nat was as happy to be getting rid of her as she was to be getting rid of Nat.

She got on a plane. She flew. She landed. However, when, after those few important hours, Alice spotted her father across the crowd at the airport, she unaccountably felt the tying and tightening of a knot in her stomach: She suddenly knew something was not going to be right. She watched her dad looking for her in the crowd, and she saw that his face held not the tender excitement he had manifested for Alice's summertime visit; now, her father scanned the faces in a more perfunctory manner, unsmiling, unexpectant. When her dad *did* see her, he gave a small smile and a little businesslike wave, before tucking his head and dodging through the crowd. But when he arrived and Alice flung herself into what she imagined would be an embrace of pure joy, she instead found herself left to hang by the arms from her father's stiffened neck as he bent to take her luggage.

"Whoa!" said her dad. "We don't want all these people thinking I've got myself a sweetie-pie!"

"Why not?" said Alice, only partially masking the fact that she was hurt. "What's wrong with sweetie-pies?"

"Well, there's a time and a place for everything," said her dad mysteriously. By then he had picked up Alice's two suitcases and, without exactly looking right at her but kind of smiling in a general manner in her direction, he made his way, with Alice following, to the car. He stowed her bags in the trunk, opened her door, then got himself situated behind the wheel, all without returning Alice's hug.

"Are you even glad?" Alice asked.

"About—oh! Yes, sure! Sure, honey-love, yes, very happy, Nana too, can't wait to settle you in and all that, though I must say it is rather sudden and, well, we *will* have to kind of tiptoe around for a while until we get Nana comfortable with the whole idea, because she's still kind of in shock about Pops's death and she did just buy the house and hasn't really settled in *herself* yet—"

Alice's face went awry. "We—what do you mean? We're—are we going to be living with *Nana*?"

"Well, yes, I mean, of course we are. That's where I live now, just kind of a boarder really, and you'll be another right along with me. She owns the house, you see, and I'm, I'm there with her." Her father said all of this while twisting and turning to see what he needed to see in his various mirrors before backing out of the parking space and eventually finding his way onto the highway.

"But what about your cool little apartment?" said Alice.

"Well, Alice, I mean, you know, that *was* just an apartment, no equity or anything, and Nana bought this house and invited me to move in and, well, it hardly made sense then to pay for that apartment too. After Pops died she sold the big house and wanted something much smaller, see. But there's plenty of room! Don't worry, we'll squeeze in. Plenty of room for, well, for all of us."

Alice noted that her father sounded far from convinced. Alice wondered how convinced her grandmother was. And she thought about why she felt so dejected to learn that she and her dad would be living with his mother.

Obviously, gone was the our-little-hideaway feeling that her father's small apartment had taken on. She would be sharing her dad with another person. But she had always done that growing up, sharing him with her own mother. Okay, no apartment, and okay, some more sharing—so what?

It came down to how she felt about her grandmother, really. And she was afraid she had never much cared for Nana. But she felt sorry for her since her husband had died. Nana had always seemed devoted to Pops. But she never seemed to have any devotion left over, no classic cheery granny-ness, no pie-baking and cookie-making, for her only grand-child. That was fine, Alice could understand it; after all, Alice had adored her grandfather, too—but it left her feeling her grandmother had barely noticed her all these years. Alice's father had once come upon Alice when she happened to be feeling chilled after an encounter with her grandma and had put his arm around Alice's shoulder and said, "You know, she was that kind of mother, too."

"What do you mean?" Alice had asked.

"I mean she was kind of a cold fish as moms go," her dad said with a laugh.

"But—but you're her *son*!" Alice had said.

Her dad had shrugged.

In trying now to think about her grandmother, Alice kept thinking instead about her grandfather, who had understood her the way her own dad did, but who had been nuttier, collaborating with her on outlandish inventions, building tree houses higher than any parent would sanction, taking over garden plots to try to grow bizarre hybrids they grafted in their private "laboratory." When her grandfather had died earlier in the year, Alice had learned an important lesson: that you could lose something forever without granting permission for it to go.

Some of Alice's misgivings about her grandmother, and their living arrangements, were happily dispelled when Nana greeted her granddaughter warmly and took her to "your room," which was actually the old attached garage off the basement. But the walls, she assured Alice, were good, sound double brick, and, what with the thin paneling she herself had tacked up to waist level, it really *was* a comfy room, was it not? She pointed out the low, single bed on the metal frame, and the small desk made of boards and bricks, and the one small, empty bookshelf that Alice knew was supposed to be a particular welcoming sign, as her grandmother *did* know Alice loved to read and would need a place to keep "your favorites."

Alice assured her the room was just perfect, and thanked her profusely for taking her in on such short notice. This seemed to make her grandmother and her father uneasy, so Alice quickly dropped the subject of gratitude and began to unpack some of her books, loading up the little shelf. That made them much more comfortable, and soon it was time for dinner.

The next day her father took her to the school she was to attend, which seemed a nice enough place, but which in fact, she was to spend only six official school days attending, because within the week Alice had begun to develop a harsh cough and congestion of breath, in the chill of her garage room.

The fact is, she became ill very fast. She tried to hide it, but the cough was constant. She ran an on-and-off low-grade fever, too, and within a short while was spending most of her days strangely worn out in her cold bed, while her grandmother clumped around the floors above, silent except for her footfalls. For lunch she left Alice a portion of whatever she herself ate, on a tray at the head of the stairs to the main house; usually it was a bowl of canned tomato soup.

Her father called in the old man who had been Alice's pediatrician long ago when Alice was a toddler, and although the old doctor was delighted to see Alice, he did not give much help in diagnosing what was wrong with her. "A little croup that's going around" was the sum of his wisdom. He actually gave Alice a lollipop at the end of his "exam," as if Alice had been a good girl by holding still.

Eventually the dankness of the garage was noticed by Alice's father, and after some arguing that she heard only as indistinct tones through the ceiling, Alice was moved upstairs to share her father's room.

But that only made her cough more audible in Nana's room, and her by now sickly presence more grating to her grandmother, against whose flurries of temper her father took shorter and shorter stands.

It did not seem to go on for very long, especially when Alice considered that she had expected it to go on forever. But here she was, back with her mother again, listening to her bourbon-scented vows as she swore fealty to the God who had restored her "baby" to her. In the wings, as soon as this bronchial business had been dispatched, was Sergeant Husband, waiting, arms crossed, to welcome back the weird kid who had indisputably now become a "sicko."

SEVEN

"SO LET ME MAKE SURE I've got this right," said Rex brightly one afternoon a couple of weeks after her arrival. "This guy's basically King of the Rednecks and he understands you about as well as that dead plant on the windowsill does."

Alice nodded. She didn't trust herself to speak much: That morning, she had been told her bronchitis was under control and she would be free to go home the next morning, and she did not want to cry in front of a dying kid. So she tried to restrict herself to nods and head shakes.

"Plus he hates you to boot, right? Thinks you're weird and prissy because you don't kill squirrels with your slingshot and stuff—you don't have to tell me. Really wishes you weren't around to get in the way when he puts the moves on your mom, but if you have to be there you ought to at least be a *real* kid, like a junior redneck with pigtails."

Alice risked saying, "You got it."

"And you don't want to live under those conditions, especially if you toss in a mom who's loaded most of the time, if you'll pardon my mentioning it? Of course you don't want to. Who would?"

Without waiting for an answer, Rex, pacing excitedly, said, "So, why not just stay *here*? It's what I do."

Alice gave a bitter laugh. "I have no idea how to fake a fatal illness, Rex," she said. "And anything short of that wouldn't be enough to keep me here."

"No? Are you sure?"

Alice realized that, actually, she *wasn't* sure. Of course the idea of hanging safely on to the congenial hospital routine had appealed to her. The two kids were left under the minimal supervision of a nurse who doubled as a standup comic. No one really "belonged" in the hospital, and the neutrality of this situation seemed like a kind of salvation. But things were, as always, out of her hands. The doctor said, "You can go." Her mother said, "Come home to Momma." And so she was to go. Was she not? Out of her hands.

Just then a nurse's aide wheeled in the lunch trays. Rex started eating immediately. But for some reason Alice took a moment, looking at the food on the tray. She looked at her hand, which had picked up a fork prior to using it to cut and spear a piece of Salisbury steak. That fork—it was literally not "out of her hands" now, was it?

Carefully, slowly, she laid the fork back down, into exactly the spot it had come from. Rex, chewing, looked up. "Hey," he said, "what's the matter? You not hungry?" Then he noticed Alice's involuntarily shrewd eyes, and stopped chewing. He swallowed his steak, and smiled.

"You clever witch," he said. "You look like you just discovered the formula for Coca-Cola, or how to dimple golf balls, or something equally important. And you did, didn't you? You discovered something important. You discovered that you were not in the least hungry."

Alice smiled close-lipped, crossed her arms, and nodded.

Rex grinned. "I bet you're not going to be hungry for a *long* time. Am I right?"

Alice, still smiling tightly, raised her eyebrows and gave a shrug. Then she nodded.

"Ingenious," said Rex. "You know, I think it might just work."

EIGHT

THE MOST DIFFICULT part had been simply explaining to her mother. She was drunker than usual, and could not seem to understand: Alice *could* eat, the food they brought was perfectly acceptable, but she *wasn't* going to eat? But—that meant she'd *starve*. No, the doctor explained wearily, that was why she was going to have this needle in her arm twenty-four hours a day, dripping concentrated glucose, to keep her tissues manufacturing the necessary amino acids and so on. He just as wearily explained that psychological tests had shown clearly that the girl did not suffer from any of the clinical eating disorders, such as bulimia and anorexia nervosa.

Alice's mother continued to look dumbfounded. But that stuff coming through that nasty needle—that wasn't *food*, she said thickly. Why wouldn't they bring her real *food*?

Finally the doctor left in a huff of disgust, both at her mother's drunken denseness and at Alice's arrogance in pulling such a stunt while under his care. "I cannot discharge a patient who is malnourished and since it has been more than thirty-six hours since your last meal you are technically malnourished, so here we are. Very clever. Well, it's not *my* concern—nothing pulmonary about it, so I'm out of here. But you watch it, Ms. Starve Yourself. Trouble comes quicker than you or the great Rex over there might think." Eventually the nurse took Alice's loopy mother away, downstairs to where Nat was smoking Pall Malls in the car and waiting, and she and Rex were left alone.

Alice was exuberant. "I did it!" she said. "I freaking *did* it! They can't *touch* me! All I have to do is keep *giving up* something, and I'm golden. And anybody can give up something. It's not what I have to *do*—it's what I have to *not* do, and what could be easier?"

Rex seemed oddly subdued by comparison. "The doctor, when he was jamming in the glucose drip, said something about not wanting to deprive you of your shot at martyrdom." He looked at Alice carefully.

"And I told him I had no interest in becoming a martyr," Alice said, cheeks still flushed with her victory. "I told him that if I went to that so-called *home* of Nat's and Mother's I would become a martyr, that *that* was martyrdom. But he didn't get it. Sometimes I think the only thing they want to understand around this place is living and dying. Either you're one, or the other, and whatever there is in between doesn't matter."

"Welcome to the world," said Rex. "Hope you can stay awhile."

NINE

ONE AFTERNOON ALICE woke up and found herself staring into a pair of oversized brown eyes with a ludicrously knowing look to them. She took her time seeing that the eyes belonged to a man about forty, apparently a doctor, as he wore a white cotton jacket like a sports coat. But the coat was the only sign of medical authority—the man wasn't wearing a stethoscope, and none of the jacket's pockets bulged with medical paraphernalia.

"A shrink," said Alice. "Got to be."

"I hope I didn't startle you awake," the man said in a quiet, slightly high-pitched voice, the pleasant honesty of which did a lot to make the look in his eyes seem more like a physical effect due to their size, and less like a smug assumption of wisdom. He put out his hand. "I'm Dr. Jonathan. And I am indeed a shrink."

Alice shook the hand. But she still said, "Is saying 'I'm Dr. Jonathan' like saying 'I'm Captain Bob, kids!' Or is your last name really Jonathan?"

The man laughed. "All right—let me do it over. Hi! I'm Dr. Archibald, kids!"

Alice was impressed. "Your name is really Archibald Jonathan?"

The man nodded.

"Do you ever get mixed up and introduce yourself as 'Jonathan Archibald'?"

"Frequently," the man said with a straight face. "Sometimes I go so far as to say 'Jonny Archie.'"

Alice smiled.

"I'm here to figure out all of the hidden stuff about why you're not eating, but you can save me a lot of trouble," Dr. Jonathan said. "*Is* there a lot of hidden stuff, or should we just stick to the stated program?"

"Nice of you to ask," Alice said. "It *is* just what I've said."

"That you don't want to go home."

"Not to *that* home."

Dr. Jonathan put a hand on each knee and pushed

himself upright out of the chair he had pulled up to Alice's bedside. Alice noted that he was an unusually small man, probably about 5 feet 4, maybe 105 pounds.

"Yes," Dr. Jonathan sighed, reading her look. "It's very difficult buying clothes. For reasons I don't want to examine too closely, I refuse to buy anything in a Boys' department, though in fact I'm a perfect size twenty." He held up a sleeve, and Alice noticed for the first time that the sleeve had been rolled up a few times, though it still extended over the man's wrist. She also noted that the rolled part had been pressed and starched like the rest of the coat, as if the cuff were just a fashion option.

Alice said, "I'd have a heck of a time right now, too, especially with pants. My waist must measure about the circumference of a grapefruit." she said. "Not that it matters, but I bet I'm hideous. I was already pretty thin when I started this thing."

Dr. Jonathan's eyes zeroed in almost alarmingly. "Yes. So you were. And actually, that's rather important, isn't it? Because if you had been plump, well, then we all might have misconstrued your . . . 'thing' as a mere diet. Something merely *practical*."

Alice half-smiled. "Oh? And how do 'you all' *construe* it now?"

"Oh, well! As something quite otherwise—as something quite radical, really!"

Alice frowned. "Then you're still not getting it. I'm not—if you knew me, you'd know I'm not the kind of kid who does radical things. I'm just not radical at all."

"No?" Dr. Jonathan said, as if willing to believe her, but still needing assurance.

Alice sighed. "No. But I understand how you couldn't be aware of that. I mean, here I am, someone who has refused to eat for almost six weeks and has lost—what? How much is it by now? How many pounds, exactly?"

Dr. Jonathan narrowed his eyes a bit and touched his chin. "Now, isn't that interesting? That you presume I would know the exact number of pounds while you yourself apparently do not."

Alice smiled. "Are you going to try to tell me you *don't* know the exact number?"

Dr. Jonathan shook his head. "Oh, not at all—I wouldn't lie to you. I do know, to the ounce. But why would you be so sure of it?"

Alice, with a quick crankiness, said, "Because it's *you* guys who are the counters, the measurers, the ones who say 'When you reach this number, then blah blah blah has this percentage chance of happening to you.'"

"Which you find kind of . . . vulgar? This reduction to numbers of something so . . . complex?"

Alice shook her head in exasperation. "No! The opposite! Making something complex out of what I'm doing, which is so simple."

Dr. Jonathan nodded. "Yes. Certainly. Just . . . not eating! What could be simpler? I see what you mean. But"—he wrinkled his forehead—"the statement your simple action makes, and you must forgive me for being a little shrinkish here, the statement can mean so many things, you see?"

Alice was stony. "What 'statement'?"

"Well, it's first of all a matter of what *you* believe you're stating, isn't it? Which, as you invite me to guess, I imagine to be something along the lines of 'See? I can take over, all by myself.' Whereas, *I* think you're saying, 'Won't someone listen to me, take me seriously, love me?'" His large eyes searched Alice's openly. "Am I close?"

Alice, still stony, thought for a moment. Then she seemed to relax a small amount, enough to concede with a nod: "Fair enough. Close enough."

Dr. Jonathan looked grateful, but went on to say, "Yet this matter of not knowing the number of pounds lost—I mean, it *is* your body, is it not? I mean, that's largely the point? *Your* body? *Your* life?"

Alice nodded aggressively. "It sure is mine."

Dr. Jonathan nodded with her. "Yes. It sure is." He waited a moment, then said, "Yet you aren't interested in the—well, the numbers."

"The numbers—it's just more of you men making a big deal out of something simple."

The doctor considered her and the point. Then he nodded and said, "I can see it your way, this matter of 'simplicity.' But only if I see—well, the end of your life as something simple. Which to me means seeing your life itself as something simple, and although I don't know you well, that's too far for me to go. I do not believe your life is a simple thing. Is it, now?"

Alice, searching for words, seemed half amused, half aghast. "But—what—why—why would you, not you yourself but anyone, think I am trying to, to *reach* the end of my life? I mean, it's precisely because I know what I can and cannot live with, because I care about being *happy* in my life, that I am doing this!"

Dr. Jonathan waited a moment, then asked quietly, "And do you imagine you can do this forever?"

"'Forever?'" Alice echoed, with a sudden weariness. "I certainly hope not! That sounds so awful and long! And what does it mean, anyway?" Then, before the doctor could reply, her eyes widened and she said, a notch more softly, "Oh. Sure. I see."

"Yes. I'm afraid the medical community has only one way of defining 'forever.' And, as you point out, it is not at all what you are aiming for." The doctor nodded as if in complete agreement and, putting out his hand again—a hand not much larger than Alice's—as if to signal the end of the talk, but also perhaps almost a deal to shake on, said, "It isn't what we want either, you see. Please forgive me for tiring you so. And thank you for speaking so frankly with me."

Alice shook the hand, and did not try to hide that she was tired.

Wearily, she closed her eyes and practically whispered, "You *are* a shrink, aren't you? Well, 'bye now, you're okay."

"'Bye, Alice," said the doctor. "And thank you. I'll take that as an opening to ask if I may come back?"

Alice closed her eyes and gave an almost invisible shrug. "Fine with me. I'll be here."

"Yes," said Dr. Jonathan, "that's your point, isn't it? Anyway, Alice, nice to meet you."

"And you."

The doctor nodded, and left.

When Alice told Rex that Dr. Jonathan had stopped by, Rex said, "Him? He's all right. But he's still a shrink."

"Meaning what?"

"Meaning don't be surprised when he sneaks up on you and tells you what everything you do *means*." Rex laughed.

Dr. Jonathan came back twice that week. Mostly, they discussed her hallucinations, in detail, almost studiously. But during his third visit, Alice asked the doctor a question.

"Hey—did my other doctors ask you, like, about what I told you? So they could look for signs or something, the way they look for numbers?"

"Well," said Dr. Jonathan, wrinkling his forehead, "yes, they did ask me. And, yes, there are predictive signs they are on the lookout for—certain things they might interpret to indicate upcoming changes in your . . . health."

"And you told them? What did they say?"

The wrinkle deepened in Dr. Jonathan's forehead, accompanied by a small frown. "Well, to tell the truth, I am rather prickly on the issue of confidentiality. I'm afraid it often brings me into conflict with my colleagues, who feel I ought to . . . share more of the things my patients reveal, for the sake of my patients. This— well, this was an occasion for one of those conflicts."

Alice's eyes grew wide. "You can't mean you refused to tell them?"

With the same frown, Dr. Jonathan nodded. "I'm afraid that's exactly what I did. So I'm sorry, I cannot relate to *you* what *their* reaction was. But I did strike a kind of devil's bargain with them, and if you like I'll strike it with you, too, to be fair."

"Let's hear it."

"Well, a psychiatrist is of course a medical doctor as well as an analyst," Dr. Jonathan said, "a fact my colleagues allow themselves to overlook at times. So I am perfectly capable of noting any key 'signs' that might indicate a change they would wish to be alerted to, because it might mean you were coming up on some—well, trouble, or at least some serious weakening. So I agreed to let them know if any such medical signs came up, without at all revealing the substance of our talks."

Alice thought for a moment, then said, "Sounds fair to me."

"Good."

"Well?" Alice said. "Are there, so far? Signs, I mean? Have any of them 'come up'?"

Dr. Jonathan looked at her for a moment, then gave a small sigh. "I'm afraid a couple have, yes. I might even say a few."

Alice nodded, and swallowed hard. She did not ask for a more elaborate explanation. Dr. Jonathan did not give one. After a few moments, they resumed what Alice called "the catalogue of freakiness." When they had finished, and had shaken hands, Alice said, "May I ask you something?"

"Of course."

Alice looked at the ceiling. "Do you think I'm nuts?"

"You mean—well, no. I do not. Not at all."

She looked at him. "But there's something you're not saying."

Dr. Jonathan frowned and thought. At last he said, "Let's just say that I think I understand your intentions pretty well and insofar as I am any judge, I find them to be completely reasonable, respectable, even honorable. And remembering that it *is* your life, *your* life, all the same, I hope your, well, *control* of things is not lost to you. I hope that . . . certain dangers don't take over from you, don't rip that control out of your hands, quite without your consent. If these dangers *did* take over—well, then you could be seen as having thrown your life away, which *does* strike one as being rather nuts, doesn't it?"

Alice could only nod.

TEN

WHEN YOU ARE FASTING it is easy to become self-centered. Alice figured this out—after all, her body, and what it was not doing, was the entire focus of an increasingly numerous and increasingly frantic series of tests, speculations, predictions, examinations, by specialists in "eating disorders." One day, when her mother was sober and still talking to her, Alice made a huge effort to explain that she had no interest in "wasting away" but rather wanted to hang on as long as possible—which she secretly believed was indefinitely—to a life away from Nat and, yes, from her mom's own drunkenness. Her mother listened to Alice's rationale, but at the end she came back to the fact that, whatever the reasons, her daughter *was* wasting away, and no mother could stand to see that happen, not when it didn't *have* to.

It is easy to become self-centered when you spend most of your time drifting in and out of either hallucinations or that mental wasteland of clarity without content, which Alice could choose to slip into, and the rest of your time pinching your arm to see if you can find any fat beneath your skin.

It is easy to become self-centered when your only friend is absent for long periods, wandering around a large hospital doing mysterious things or getting mysterious treatments, sometimes lasting all night, which leave him sleeping all day, and when that friend, awake, seems so self-sufficient and chipper that he doesn't really need to call you back from your increasing hallucinations.

But one morning Alice returned from the bathroom and was surprised to find Rex standing at one of the room's four low windows, looking out, not turning with a raised non-eyebrow and an arch word, as might have been expected. In fact, Rex was not turning at all, though Alice knew her entry had been heard. Quietly, Alice put down her toothbrush and towel, and waited.

After a few minutes, without turning around,

Rex said, "You remember how I let you believe you saw through me, saw how I didn't really believe 'it' would ever really happen to me? How I thought the whole fatality thing was a crock dreamed up by a doc whose guess was no better than mine?"

Alice said, "I knew you were passing gas. But at the time it fit who you wanted to be."

Rex nodded. "Well," he said, "I will admit this only once, and I will admit it only to you, but—the fact is, I know it *is* going to happen. Worse, in fact. I know it's already happening."

"Do you feel—"

"I feel just fine, thank you. Same as ever," Rex said. "The difference is, it gets harder and harder to keep forgetting, you know?" He kept looking out the window, but by raising her own head, Alice could see Rex was silently weeping, with his eyes only, the tears just rolling out. "Hey, you know what?" he said finally. "I mean, this sounds really dumb, but sometimes, I just want my mommy."

"Rex," Alice said, "forgive me, but your mommy, when she visits you, doesn't seem to bring a whole lot of warmth, certainly not enough to answer the call you're making right now."

"My dad was a physician, did I ever tell you? A gastrointestinal guy. But he quit his practice the day after he got the news about me. As if it were *his* fault, as if a *good* doctor wouldn't have let such a thing creep up inside his own son." Rex gave a single laugh, and shook his head. "I'd think it was arrogant if it weren't so sincere. So now, you know what he's doing? He manages a shoe store in a mall. A *shoe store*."

"Your mother always wears black, like she's already in mourning," said Alice. "I'm sorry, but I think it's gruesome."

"She thinks it shows *respect*," said Rex, still not turning around.

"For *what*? For the *disease*? Give me a break."

Rex continued to stare out the window. Then he turned toward a bed not far from his own and started pulling cardboard cartons out from under it. "I think maybe you should give my mom a break," he said without rancor. When he had pulled four boxes out, he used the toe of a sneaker to flip open a lid. Alice could see that the whole thing was full to the top with sappy, sentimental, store-bought cards with flowers all over them.

"Are those—"

Rex nodded. "Get-well cards. 'Cheer cards.' 'Encouragement cards.' Four boxes of them. I get one a day." He smiled. "Usually in a colored envelope, an *awful* color."

Alice stared at the collection of paper petunias and lilies and roses curved around rhymed messages written in flowing script. "But—why, Rex?"

Rex shrugged. "Best I can figure is, that the horror of it has just kind of made Mommy mute. So she goes to the Hallmark store and finds that her grief has already been put into nice words, that other people must have these feelings too, or they wouldn't print these things, see? So, like, what she can't say by herself, she can kind of transfer from these *pre-expressed* cards to me. And hope I feel it as if I were the only person in the world getting one of them."

"And do you? It's all right to tell me—I won't mock you, Rex," said Alice.

Rex used a foot to shove the boxes back beneath the bed, one after the other. "I guess sometimes I do," he said. "I guess sometimes I want to. I want to feel that someone cares." He laughed bitterly. "Boy, *that* sounds like one of these cards."

"You've got someone who cares as long as I'm here, Rex," Alice blurted. "I'll give you whatever you need. Really!"

Rex laughed again. "Oh, yes? Will you, now? Not that I don't appreciate the offer, Alice, but have you thought about what you're promising? To give me 'whatever I need'?"

He turned and faced her now, and his face was blotchy. He was not smiling. "Listen, you with your self-induced stoned-out lightness and brightness and whatever hallucination you're grooving on today. I am *dying*. One day, before too very long, certainly before it would naturally happen to you, I am going to *die*. To die, girl. And at that time I will need only *one* thing, and that thing is *life*. You can't give me that, Alice. Nobody can, okay? It is *impossible for you to help me*, understand?"

He looked at her a moment longer, then strode out of the room. Before he got to the door, Alice managed to say, "Maybe not, Rex—but I promise I'll do whatever I can. I promise. Whatever it is."

Then the doors swung to.

ELEVEN

ONCE, BEFORE HER MOTHER had stopped talking to her, she came to visit Alice, took a look at her, and said, "Jesus. You look like that dog in the kids' book, what's his name, Ribsy."

"Good," said Alice. "Ribsy is extremely cool."

Her mom had her magazine out. "Yeah? Listen, Alice—why do you just *have* to be a complete fool?"

"At least I'm not dying, like Rex," she said, thinking the melodrama of it would get to her mom. But no.

"I'm sure you could work that out if you wanted to," her mother said, flipping pages. "You're the gal holding all the strings."

Alice said, "What would you do if I died?"

"Attend your funeral, probably," her mother said, not looking up.

TWELVE

So heavy! Her body was stone, pressing down on the mattress, squeezing the breath out of her. Then when she could stand it no longer, the stone would lighten a little, and her body would be made of sand. That was only a little more comfortable, but then it would transform into something like plastic, and she knew she would get there. Sure enough, the plastic changed too, into a kind of rubbery foam, then the bubbles of the foam became lighter, until they were like the ones you blow out of soapy water, but dry. She began to rise off the mattress, and she knew it was okay, she was on her way, the lightness was coming. The gas in the bubbles got lighter and finer, and the skin of the bubbles stretched thinner and thinner. Finally, the bubbles popped and she was that light gas itself, rising. But even the gas was too heavy, and it faded away. After that, there was nothing to do but vanish.

THIRTEEN

O NE NIGHT ALICE WOKE UP and realized two things. First, she was not having a hallucination: She was just right there in her bed in the huge children's ward, alert, weighing whatever she weighed, seeing whatever was before her. Her second revelation was that she had been awakened by the departure from the room, here in the middle of the night, of Rex.

Immediately Alice decided to follow him. She had long been curious about what Rex did during the night—not curious enough to ask, and too self-centered to do any real investigation. But here was her chance.

Alice swung her legs over the side of the bed. Two

steps dragging her wheeled IV pole shocked her with the realization that she was terribly weak; she looked around and located the dim shape of a wheelchair along one wall. Once she had collapsed into its seat, looped her glucose bag over a handle on the back, taken a couple of breaths, and spun the wheels toward the double doors, she felt all right. But the wheeling was hard work, too, and she had to keep taking breaks—lots of breaks—as she went.

By peering through the space between the doors Alice could see that a single nurse was sleeping at the nurse's station twenty feet up the hall. Blessing the silence of her rubber wheels, Alice spun past with barely a sound and was off into the main body of the hospital. Rex and any signs of his passage were gone, but Alice had faith in her instincts—she would find him, somewhere. In the meantime, maybe she would wander a little.

Alice was shocked to find that a hospital is not an especially good place to wander, that it's full of people in great discomfort, people who tend to sleep poorly and cry out in the night. She passed many doors from which terrible noises emerged. She rolled as fast as she could down hallways as they appeared to her right and left.

Then she took a left at one hallway, and at the end

she found some French doors that opened to a silent bump from her wheels, and suddenly she was on a tiled patio open to the sky, bordered by a white waist-high balustrade that seemed to glow in the dark with a kind of comforting magic. Alice wheeled to the center of the space and stopped, looking up at the bright night sky full of stars. After a moment, she realized she was not alone on the patio.

"What the devil has got ahold of *you?*" said the scratchy voice of an old man, and when Alice looked down from the sky and toward the voice, she saw another wheelchair, this one drawn up against the balustrade, with the paleness of a face turned her way in the moonlight.

"Excuse me," she started to say.

"You're welcome out here," said the old man. "Especially as you look like you got about two weeks left in you."

"What do you mean?" said Alice.

"Oh, it's denial, is it? They got all these fancy words for not wanting to admit you're about to die. Oh, I know all about it. Natural human instinct, to stay alive as long as possible, hang on to the last moment with the fingernails, scrabbling all the way." Alice saw the head shake slowly. "Well, they'd say you're in denial, most likely. You look like something pulled out of Dachau in 1945. What is it? The Big C? Eating you up from inside? Maybe from the stomach? They're finding a lot more Big C in the stomach these days; must be all that crap you kids eat instead of real food."

"I don't have—" But for reasons of weariness she decided against explaining. So she settled on another truth, and just said, "Yes, it's the stomach."

"Too bad," said the old man. "I hear it hurts at the end."

"Not especially," she said. "In fact, not at all."

The head nodded. "Denial," he said in his prickly voice, "for sure. But it's okay. Out here we can deny whatever the hell we want."

"What—I mean, why are *you*—"

"Renal," the man said. "You know what that means?"

"Yes."

"You never know if the kids these days learn all the words," he said.

"Both?" said Alice. "I mean, you have two kidneys—"

"Lot of good two of 'em did *you*," said the man a little peevishly, "if you'll pardon my saying so. You look like a housecat just had a bath and didn't get dried yet. I hope you got to use your stomach a *little*."

"Oh, I got to use it a *lot*," said Alice. Then, after a moment, she asked, "Do I *really* look that bad?"

The man studied her, not so much as if to take a longer look as if to figure out what to say. "Well," he finally said, "let me put it this way. I ain't exactly feeling too strong these days. Doc says I got a week at the most, I feel like there's fire inside from my kidneys up through the top of my head, I'm seventy-nine years old—but the way you look, I feel like I could wheel over there and poke my finger right through you anywhere on your body. Paper. What's that Japanese art where they do all that folding?"

"Origami," said Alice.

"Well, friend, you don't look like you'd offer as much resistance as one of those birds or whatever. Folded out of *tissue*."

"Thanks for telling me," Alice said, somewhat shakily. "See, it's not so much denial, it's more that I don't *know*."

"I get you," said the old man. "I know what you mean, friend. You look in the mirror every day and, hey, it just looks like *you*. Not like there's a picture pasted up beside it there, Before, so you can see the After."

"Right. So you don't know how far you've gone."

"How old are you?" the man asked suddenly.

85

"Eleven," said Alice.

The head shook again. "Damn shame. Know what I regret the most for you? Know what I wish you'd get the chance for the most?"

"What?" she said.

"Kids," said the old man. "You'll never get to raise them. I'm not trying to make you feel bad or anything. But getting to raise a kid—I've got four, myself, all grown and scattered to hell and gone by now, of course—well, let me tell you, that's a privilege not to be taken lightly. It's like getting let in on all the secrets of the universe. I hate to use fancy language—what do they call it?—New Age, I hate that junk, but that's what it is. The precious secrets. You can't find out any other way. That's why people love their kids, even if they don't know it—they love them because the kids give them a peek at how it all works."

"I got to go now," said Alice.

"Hey, you're crying. I'm sorry if—"

"No, no, what you've said makes sense and it's probably true in the best sense, in the best families," she said. "Congratulations on yours."

"Sure, sure, nice talking to you. Weird, isn't it, the way you meet people in this place, knowing you both are about to check out? Hey, look, I hope it never hurts, okay?"

86

"Okay," said Alice. "So long."

"See you wherever we go next," said the old man. "Check the patios at night. I've always liked patios at night. The stars, you know. Big."

"Big," said Alice. " 'Bye."

" 'Bye."

Quickly Alice turned and left the patio, rolled down hallways without thinking, and remembered her mission only when at the end of a down-sloping passage she saw Rex. He was sitting at a spot-lit table in the middle of a dark room that looked as if its walls were lined with a jumble of tools. Three men sat with him at the table. The four of them were playing cards. As Alice watched, unseen in the darkness of the passageway, Rex took several drags on a cigar burning in an ashtray beside him, drank twice from a tumbler holding an amber liquid, and won three pots, to the good-natured consternation of his mates. After a while, Alice turned silently and hauled herself back up the passage. Somehow she found her way back to the children's ward. The nurse was still asleep, in the same position. Alice pushed through the double doors into the familiar darkness, parked the wheelchair, and made her shaky way—shakier than before—to her bed. When she awoke in the morning, Rex was deep in sleep in his bed.

FOURTEEN

ALICE NO LONGER DESCENDED from her lofty heights when she heard and smelled the entry of her mother. It even became more of a chore for her to come down and attend to Rex. But she did descend to *him*, though he often had to repeat himself a couple of times before his words penetrated the cryptic scheme of color and sound and light in which she had been floating, and she was able to decode herself into the realm of Rex's life. The silly pranks, the overdone facial expressions, the crude mockeries of voice— they all seemed less and less lively and amusing to Alice, and less worth the effort it took to watch and listen to them.

However, she answered Rex's every summons, because she always recalled her promise to him, and she never knew but that this summons might be for the aid she had sworn to give. So far it was never for that—instead, it was just that Rex needed an audience for his report on some hot nurse's sexual tastes or a technician's mix-up of some crucial cultures, or the sad tale of a paramedic dropping the pole of a stretcher bearing a severely injured car-crash victim on the way in to Emergency.

Rex knew he was calling Alice back from distances. "One day there simply won't be anything of you left to fight for," he said in a mildly scolding tone that reminded Alice of his angry reaction long ago— was it long ago?—to Bobby Q's death.

Once, stung and feeling pompous, Alice said, "I have a power that no one can take from me."

"And what is that power, oh Swami?" said Rex.

"The power," said Alice haughtily, "to give things up."

"Well, good for you, Powergirl," snapped Rex, suddenly at his most sardonic. "When I have the good fortune to give up my *life*, I'll try to let you know if I feel ultimately empowered by what otherwise would be seen as a loss. But just remember," he said, pointing a finger at Alice. "Remember—you didn't go on a hunger strike to get goofy-high and talk like a bad poet. You did it because you have your rights to defend. No one can make you live somewhere, or with somebody, that goes against your wishes, your will, your good sense. It's your *life*. Stop 'shimmering' long enough to remember: Your dad gave you the shaft because he's a wimp. Your mom's a drunk. Your stepfather's a fascist. Hold out until you find someone you can depend on, okay?"

"Okay," said Alice through a growing haze.

Rex watched closely, sighed, let his finger drop, shook his head. "Forget it. Go float and glow. But promise me one thing: Don't float away. Don't float all the way away, okay?"

"You look paler," Alice suddenly noticed.

"Yeah, well, maybe I need my tapioca. Just promise me."

"I promise. I *already* promised."

"Just drive that spaceship carefully, Captain. There are meteorites out there you don't know about."

"I will," said Alice. "See ya."

"I hope so," said Rex, and he was gone.

Alice did *not* see him again for quite a while. At about this point, about eight weeks into her hunger strike, Alice's weight reached some milestone her doctors considered ridiculously dangerous, so that suddenly most of her time was taken up receiving nutritional inducements and lectures about the perilous permanence of tissue change from deprivational damage. Even her mother, now sober day after day, joined in the pleading.

To her one day, Alice said, "Mom, people say it's bad for me but if you only knew how good it makes me *feel*—"

"Forget *that* one, honey," her mother said dryly. "I've already used it a few hundred times myself."

"Nevertheless," Alice said with her chin high, offended at her mom's amusement, "I'm not eating."

"Well, that's where we differ, because I definitely *will* be drinking."

It was her mother, three or four days later, who first told Alice about Rex. "That friend of yours, the round one, you know? I hear if you want to say cheerio you'd better hustle, because you may not have long."

Alice knew she had not seen Rex lately, but she was stunned. "You mean . . . what do you—"

"His what-you-call-it, his remission, it turned ugly in a hurry, I guess." Her mother shrugged. "He's still alive, but just barely. He's been in intensive care for the last few days hanging on."

The familiar nurse came in at that moment to check Alice's drip. Alice grabbed her feebly by the arm. "Rex?" she asked.

"You mean the kid who's *really* sick and not just pulling some starvation stunt?"

"Is he—how bad is he?"

"About as bad as he'll get," the nurse said. "Drifts in and out of a light coma, and every time he comes out of it, the doctors are surprised, if you get my meaning."

"I have to see him."

The nurse rolled her eyes and laughed. "Should have thought of that before you made yourself too weak to raise yourself up on one elbow, child," she said. "No way a starving bony thing like you is going to get into intensive as a visitor."

Alice looked at her, at her mother, then back to the nurse. She knew what she had to do—they didn't need to stare at her as if to say "Your move, girl!" She knew—but she hesitated. She couldn't help feeling she was giving something up, something she had built so carefully.

She took a deep breath and said, "Bring me something to eat, please. The most I can stand, to make me strong the fastest."

The nurse frowned. "You playing games?"

"Crackers," said Alice, "and juice, lots of apple juice."

"Oh, Alice," said her mom.

"Apple juice," said the nurse. She raised her eyebrows. "Maybe some bouillon too?"

Alice nodded.

"I know what you're trying to pull," the nurse said. "And if you think you can sip a little something and trick us into believing you're all healed up so you can get in to see that poor friend of yours, well—"

"No," said Alice. "It's not a trick. Please believe me. I won't go back to . . . not eating. I'll eat. I'll start and I won't stop again."

The nurse eyed her skeptically for what seemed like minutes. "I ought to get a slew of doctors in here," she said.

"Please," said Alice.

The nurse sighed. "I always was a sucker for romance," she said. "Apple juice and crackers and bouillon it is." Then she left.

Alice glanced in the direction of her mother. Before her mom could speak, Alice said, "Nat's still a problem. But I promised Rex I'd help him."

"Well," said her mother, "if he's any kind of friend, your staying alive will do just that."

FIFTEEN

WHEN THE NURSE, acting so authoritative no one questioned her, wheeled Alice past some curtains into the cubicle where they were keeping Rex, Alice was not surprised to see his parents already sitting there, on the far side of the bed. She had been angry at both of them before, for what she saw as their cool attitude toward their fatally ill son; now, she saw faces of true, deep misery. Her anger vanished as she greeted them, a very thin woman in a black dress, with hair scattered in tufts, and a very neat man with a perfect mustache, in a flawless business suit.

Rex was curled up on the bed with his back to them, asleep. Around him were all kinds of machines making beeps and hums, showing lines and blips proceeding across lighted screens. Rex's parents seemed to be taking great pains to remain deathly quiet, but Alice had received no instructions to tiptoe, so she spoke right out.

"Yo, the Rexter."

The man and woman started with alarm, but Rex simply opened his eyes without moving, took in the sight of Alice, closed his eyes again, and said, "Hey, Chubby. How's about a chili dog?"

"No thanks, I've eaten."

Rex raised his hairless brow without opening his eyes. Even though he wasn't moving, his stillness now seemed a matter of choice, since he was speaking freely. "Surprised you found the strength to float on down for a visit," he said. Alice realized the sentence took a lot out of the boy.

"As I said, I ate," Alice repeated. "I really did. That's the only way they'd let me in here."

Rex's eyes opened again, slightly wide in mock surprise. "No joke?" Alice shook her head. Rex went on, struggling to sound incredulous. "You spoiled your high, just to come see me before I join the great cafeteria line in the sky?"

"It was a big sacrifice," said Alice, "but that's the kind of stoned-out, air-headed pal I am, I guess."

Rex closed his eyes again. His mother had let out a kind of choking noise at the reference to the sky. "Sorry, Mom," Rex said. "Forgot. Not dying, just serving as voluntary subject to test these beep-beep toys. Not deteriorating at all, really. All an act."

In fact, Alice noted, the deterioration was striking pretty deep and pretty fast. Rex's face had lost all of its pinkness and much of its rotundity; his cheeks hung on the bones beneath them, and his nose looked like parchment stretched over a stick—in short, Alice realized with cruel irony, Rex looked more like the emaciated Alice the old man on the patio had given two weeks to live, than he looked like the old jolly Rex. His hands were drawn up under his chin as he lay on his left side, and Alice noticed as they gave an occasional tremble and involuntary jerk.

Rex spoke again, with closed eyes. "Salisbury steak and good old gray peas?"

"Not quite ready for such splendor," said Alice. "I went instead for the apple juice cocktail to start, followed by three beautifully crisp Saltines."

Rex smiled, eyes closed, and grunted. "Always had style. Tomorrow maybe risk a spoonful of mashed banana, get you through the funeral?"

"If that's what it takes. What's a mashed banana between friends? Besides a sticky mess, I mean, ha ha."

Rex's mother had begun crying quietly at the mention of a funeral, and Rex's father had closed a hand over her shoulder from behind. Rex went to sleep for about fifteen minutes, breathing regularly. None of the blips or beeps showed any change. Then suddenly he spoke again. His voice was quieter, and his style was dropping further into minimalism. Alice noticed a slowing in a few machines too.

"Think I'll fade for a while after few words," Rex said. "First—Mom?"

"Yes, darling?"

"Got a hand free, might give me one of those backrubs used to put me to sleep when I was little."

His mother leaned forward and began stroking his back lightly, tears rolling.

"Dad?"

Rex's father, sitting slightly behind his wife's shoulder, cleared his throat and said, "Yes, son? Right here."

"Been thinking. Not entirely happy with your career choice." Rex smiled; Alice could see the next line coming, and knew Rex had been anticipating its delivery with relish. "Just not sure the shoe fits, Dad."

The father smiled and swallowed hard. "No? What do you suggest instead, Rex?"

"Well," said Rex, "been thinking. Call me crazy, probably way off. But—think you'd make a great doc. Sorry, all that school, residency, bad hours. But worth it. Pretty sharp guy. Use those resources, you know?"

His father was flushed now. He said, "I'll think about it, Rex. Thanks."

"No sweat. Bones?"

"Right here," said Alice.

"Confession." The word was spoken in an even more hushed voice. She leaned close.

"Ready to receive, Rex."

"Lectured you. Told you not to give in, never let them make you live a life don't want, right?"

"That's what you said."

"Take it back now." Rex allowed himself a moment to prepare the next word: "Unequivocally. Advice now: Take any life you can. Doesn't matter. Because"—and here his voice dropped to a mere whisper—"just between us, tell you: Dying *sucks*."

"Sorry to hear it, Rex."

Rex gave a minimal shrug and said, "Can you do?" Then he closed his mouth and did not speak again for the hour Alice remained there. A nurse finally came to wheel her away. Rex's father rose and leaned across the bed to shake hands.

Alice was silent during the ride back to the ward. But when she got there she was in for a couple of surprises: There were two people in the large bright room she had gotten used to occupying alone in her reveries. One was a new kid about her age, lying on his back in a bed with each leg suspended outward from him in casts that looked like rolled pieces of white paper held up by wires.

"Hi," he said with terrific cheer. "I'm Hunter. I broke my legs."

"Could have fooled me," she said. "I'm Alice."

"Jumped out of an apple tree. Little too high I guess."

"I guess."

The other intruder, much less at ease than Hunter despite being ambulatory, was Nat, Alice's stepfather. He stared down at Alice in her wheelchair.

Nat said nothing until he had his second cigarette going, having put the first one out against the post of an unoccupied bed. Then he spoke.

"Heard you ate something. Big breakthrough, I reckon." He seemed to invite comment, but Alice said nothing. After a moment, he went on. "Anyway, I was, you know, glad and all, glad you're giving up this"—his hand gestured helplessly in the air for want of a word—"this *thing* you were up to. Glad, I mean, you'll start getting healthy again. And, you know, glad you'll get to come home." He lit another Pall Mall.

"Ah," said Alice.

"I know you don't want to," said Nat as he shook out his match and tossed it carelessly away. "I don't like you much either, frankly. We've got a few lines to draw, maybe that'll make it easier. A little give and take. What do you think?"

"Depends on who gives," said Alice, "and who takes."

Nat smiled as he exhaled. "Point taken. Point made, and taken. Pretty good one." He hesitated. "Last thing. Your mom . . . okay? I've . . . My dad was a drunk. I joined the Marines at seventeen, went to 'Nam, and shot the son of a bitch thirty-four times, though you'd have sworn he looked a lot like thirty-four little brown-skinned VC trash." He gave Alice a look. "Better not to get so bitter, okay? Look, I can tell you—it's tough being a drunk. For the rest of her life, your mom is either going to be drunk and guilty about it, or she's going to *want* to get drunk worse than anything." For some reason, he gave a quick laugh. "It's one hell of a state," he said.

"She could quit," said Alice.

"Wouldn't count on it," said Nat, with a shake of

his head. "People can't just up and quit something, you know?"

Alice half-smiled and restrained herself from commenting on all the rich irony his statement left open. "Well, we'll see, I guess."

Nat nodded fiercely. "That we will. That we will. Okay, then. I hear you've got a couple of weeks to fatten up, then we'll be back, take you home. Right?"

Alice shrugged.

"Right," said Nat, and, lighting another cigarette on the run, left in a hurry.

After a minute, Hunter called across the room, "I got a stepmother. Step-parents can be pretty weird."

"Point taken," said Alice, and they both laughed.

Then the nurse who had been wheeling Alice around came into the ward, and walked over to her. As she watched the nurse approach, Alice said, "He's dead, isn't he? He did it. Rex died."

"He's gone," the nurse admitted, as she stopped in front of Alice's wheelchair.

Alice had expected to feel something huge as a response to the anticipated news. She waited for it to come. It did not.

Suddenly it occurred to her that the huge feeling might *not* come like that, all in one piece, at one time;

instead, it might just kind of trickle through the next couple of months, maybe the next few years, possibly the rest of her life. This was a little perplexing, but also a bit of an immediate relief: She had to just let it happen.

The nurse said, "He got conscious again one last time, and he had only one thing to say, and it was a message for you. Made me promise to tell you, right to your face, right away."

"For me? What is it?" Alice demanded.

The nurse sighed slightly, and bent forward so she could look Alice in the eye a moment. "Okay," she said. "Rex said: 'Tell her all you get by giving stuff up is The Big Nothing.'" The nurse searched Alice's face as if to see whether the message had some secret meaning to her, then she sighed again and stood back up. "That was it," she said. "That's all. Word for word. I promised him. He said that, he closed up, went to sleep, and then it wasn't long."

"I guess he would know," said Alice. She thought for a moment, but no other words seemed necessary. As for *feelings*—well, you had to be alive to feel them, didn't you? She sighed, and said, "I think I would like to have some more juice and crackers."

The nurse slipped behind her and pivoted her chair expertly. "Half a glass of apple juice and maybe three Saltines. For a while, honey, you are going to be what they call a cheap date."

"I wouldn't get too smug about it," Alice said, as the nurse started to wheel her out of the ward. "I'm already thinking about a banana in the near future."

The nurse sighed. "Nobody," she said, "is ever satisfied."